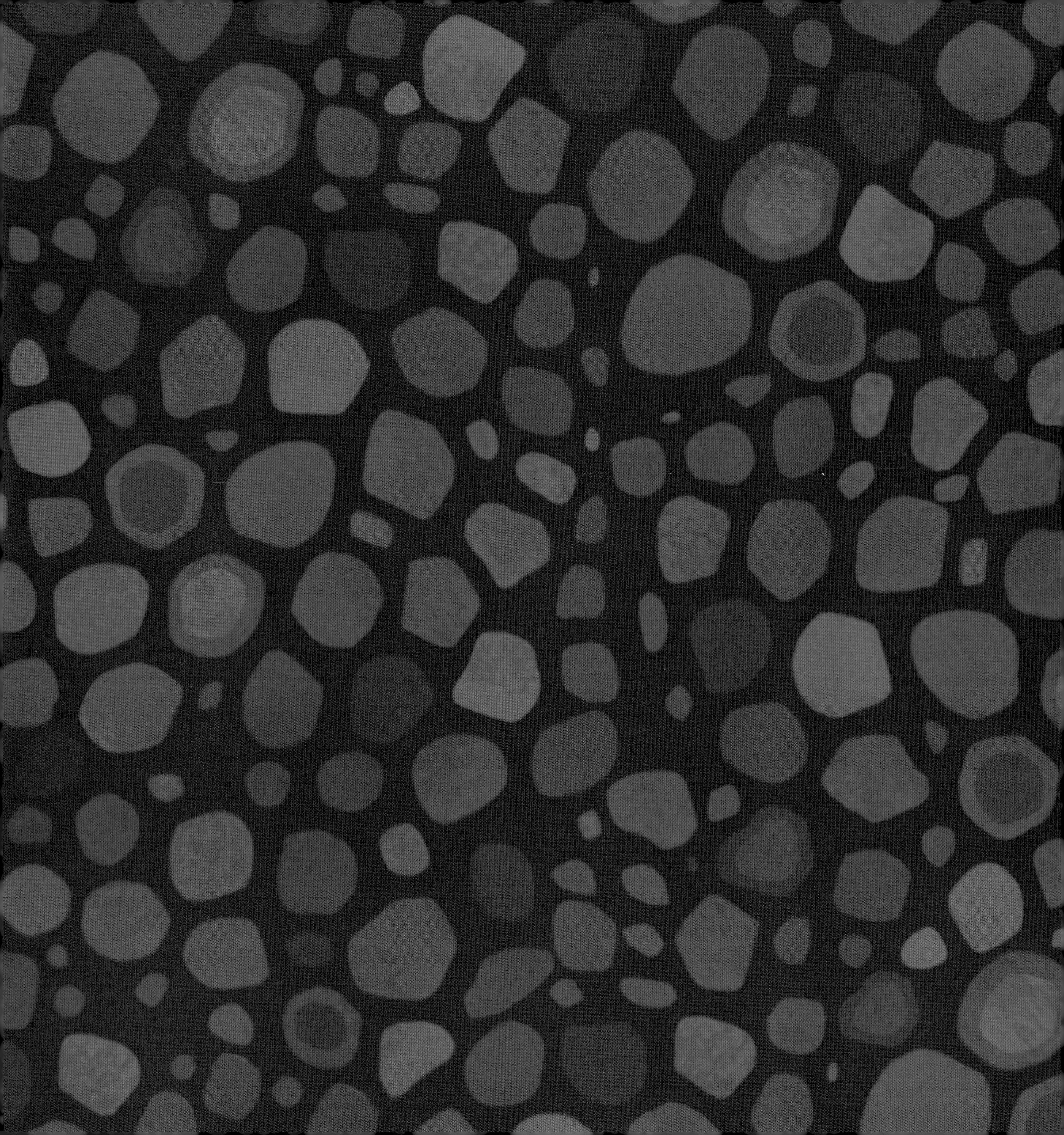

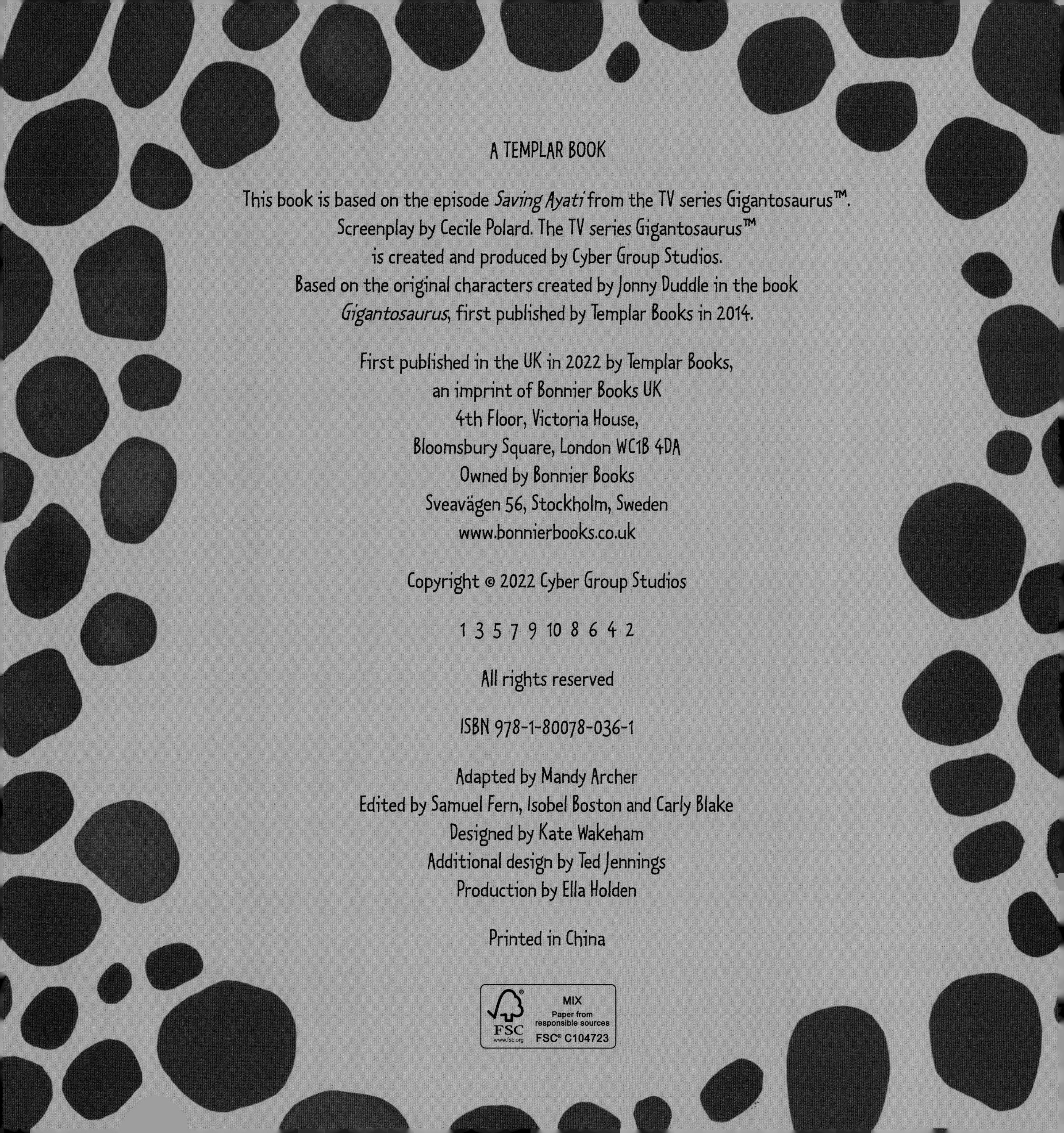

A TEMPLAR BOOK

This book is based on the episode *Saving Ayati* from the TV series Gigantosaurus™.
Screenplay by Cecile Polard. The TV series Gigantosaurus™
is created and produced by Cyber Group Studios.
Based on the original characters created by Jonny Duddle in the book
Gigantosaurus, first published by Templar Books in 2014.

First published in the UK in 2022 by Templar Books,
an imprint of Bonnier Books UK
4th Floor, Victoria House,
Bloomsbury Square, London WC1B 4DA
Owned by Bonnier Books
Sveavägen 56, Stockholm, Sweden
www.bonnierbooks.co.uk

1 3 5 7 9 10 8 6 4 2

ISBN 978-1-80078-036-1

Adapted by Mandy Archer
Edited by Samuel Fern, Isobel Boston and Carly Blake
Designed by Kate Wakeham
Additional design by Ted Jennings
Production by Ella Holden

Printed in China

FSC www.fsc.org
MIX
Paper from responsible sources
FSC® C104723

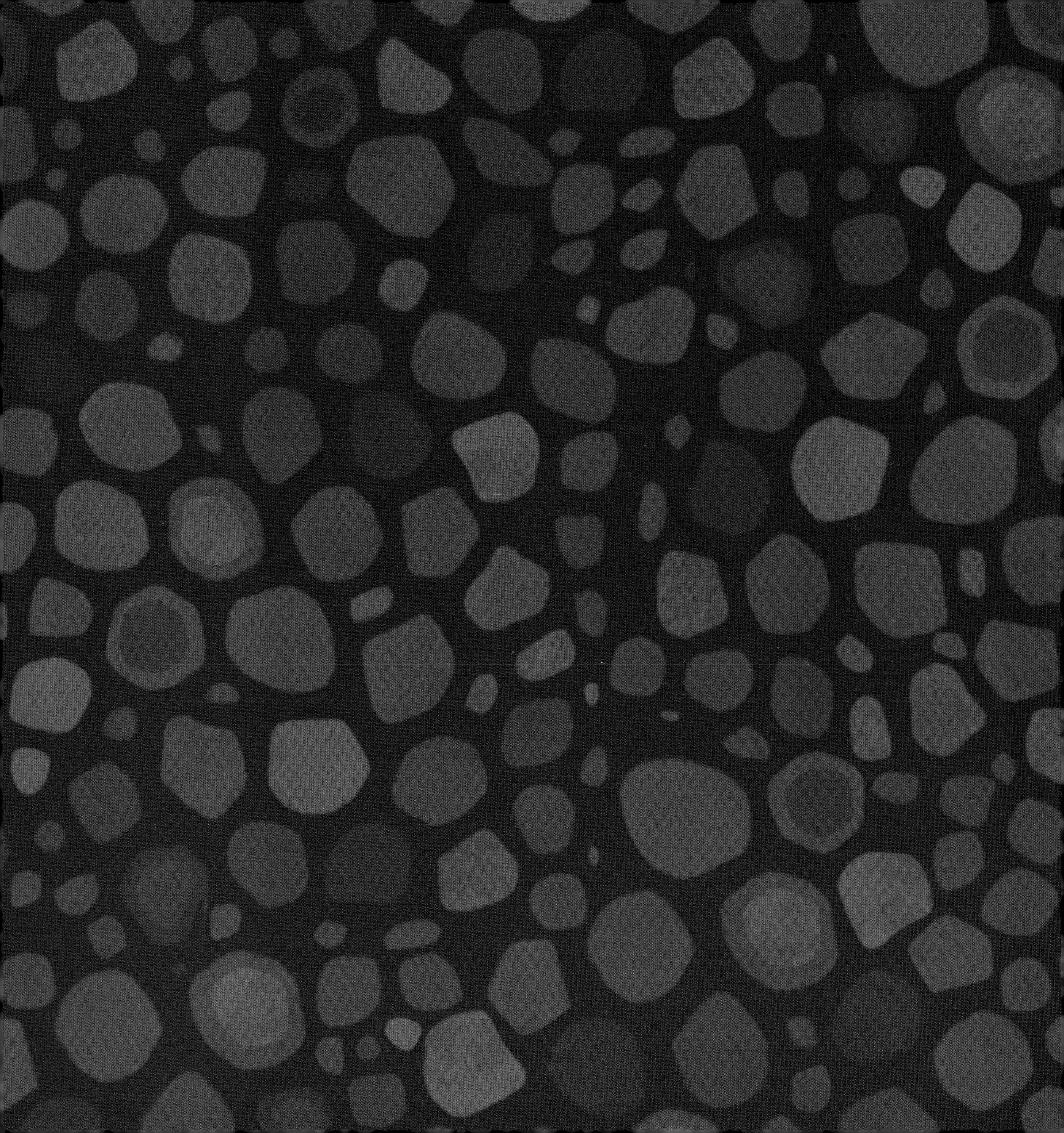

GIGANTOSAURUS™

SAVING AYATI

templar books

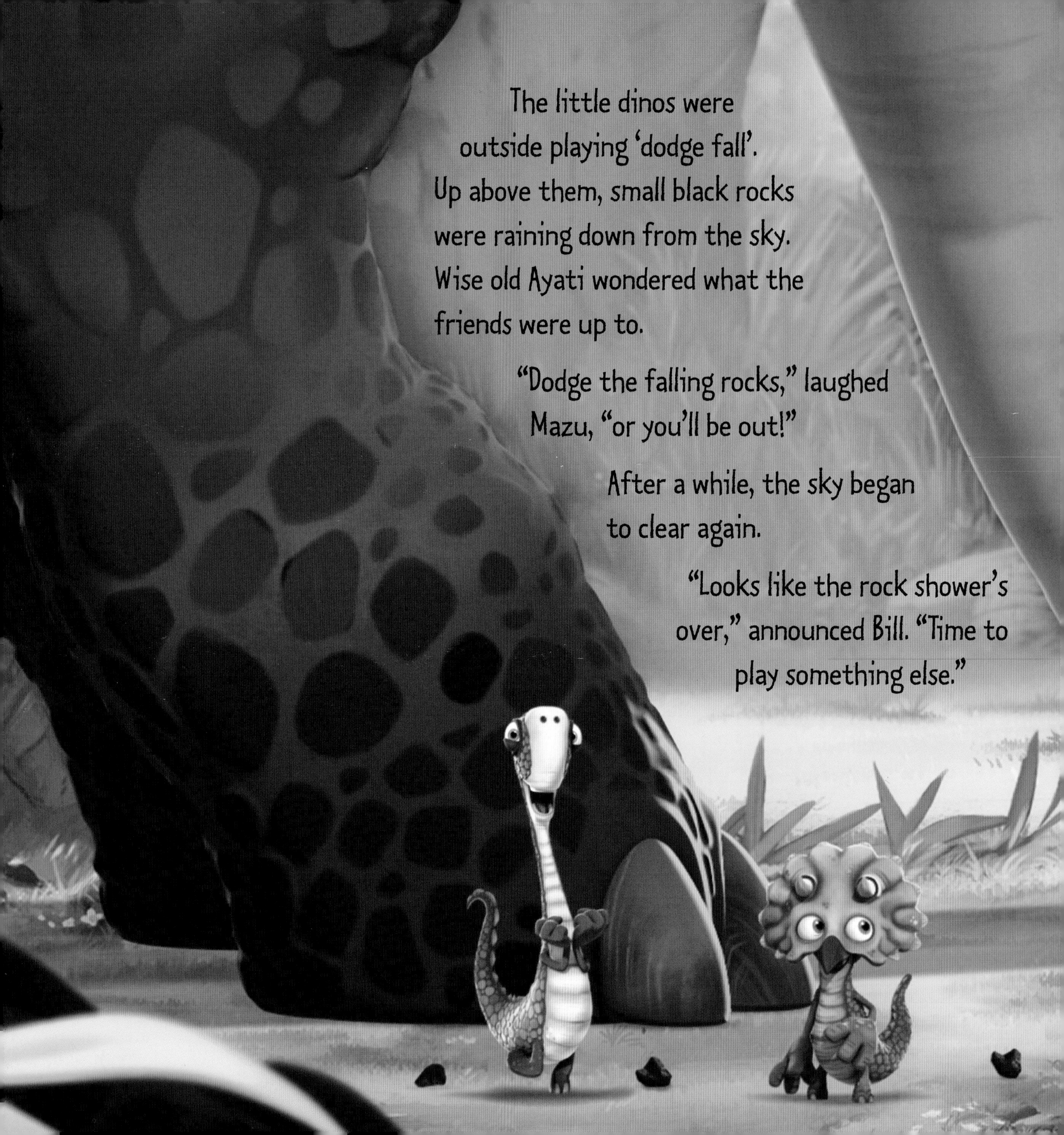

The little dinos were outside playing 'dodge fall'. Up above them, small black rocks were raining down from the sky. Wise old Ayati wondered what the friends were up to.

"Dodge the falling rocks," laughed Mazu, "or you'll be out!"

After a while, the sky began to clear again.

"Looks like the rock shower's over," announced Bill. "Time to play something else."

That looks fun!

The four friends decided to see who could think up the best new game. Bill suggested swinging, Tiny came up with bouncing and Rocky's idea was centipede-sledding on a loop-the-loop track.

"Ayati," asked Mazu, pointing to the track. "Can YOU make that shape?"

She beamed as she stretched into position. "I'm still flexible after all these years!"

Mazu cheered. "The Ayati Super-Slide is ready!" She leapt onto Ayati's back, and slid down her tail and along her neck in a loop.

Rocky and Tiny couldn't wait to have a go. Bill wasn't so sure.

WOO HOO!

"Be careful," chuckled Ayati. "You're tickling me!"

Ayati tried to adjust her body but her foot caught on a rock. She wobbled and swayed, then fell to the ground with a crash. Mazu, Tiny and Rocky were thrown through the air, straight into Bill's arms.

The little dinos were very concerned.

Their old friend was lying on her side, exhausted and helpless.

"I'm sorry," groaned Ayati. "That was one twist too many!"

"Are you hurt?" asked Bill.

"I'm fine, dear," Ayati replied, trying to smile, "but I can't get back on my feet . . ."

"Don't worry, Ayati," said Mazu. "We'll have you up again in no time!"

Mazu had an idea. "Let's all heave Ayati back onto her feet. Tiny, you can use your triceratops strength!"

Mazu, Bill and Rocky lined up by Ayati's body and Tiny by her tail. They pushed with all of their might.

Ayati's body didn't budge, but her tail began to slowly lift up from the ground.

But Tiny's arms started to tremble – Ayati's tail was too heavy to hold up.

"WATCH OUT!" bellowed Bill. He rushed over and pulled Tiny out of the way. Ayati's tail crashed to the ground, barely missing Tiny.

Poor Tiny had almost been turned into a dino pancake!

"I'm sorry," said Mazu. "This is all my fault."

"It was an accident, dear," Ayati told Mazu. "Who knew that I was so ticklish?"

A new idea popped into Mazu's head. If being tickled knocked Ayati over, maybe it could get her back on her feet, too . . .

"Let's get tickling!" shouted Mazu.

The little dinos gathered some leaves together and set to work. They each took one huge foot and tickled as fast as they could.

Ayati started to chuckle, then laugh out loud. Soon she was kicking and wriggling so hard, Bill fell off her foot. Tiny managed to catch him just in time.

TICKLE
HEE! HEE!
HA! HA!
TICKLE

“Tickling was a bad idea,” Mazu sighed. “We need to think of another way to lift Ayati up before it gets dark!”

“Thank you,” said Ayati. “I do prefer sleeping in the jungle where it’s nice and cosy.”

“Mazu will pull another idea out of that big brain of hers,” Rocky promised.

"That's it!" said Mazu. "Let's try PULLING Ayati up!"

She tied some vines all around Ayati's body, then drew her plan on a nearby rock.

"We need to wrap the vine around this tree branch and then tie it to a boulder at the top of the cliff," she explained. "If we push the boulder off the cliff, its weight will lift Ayati up!"

Rocky, Bill and Tiny nodded. "Got it!"

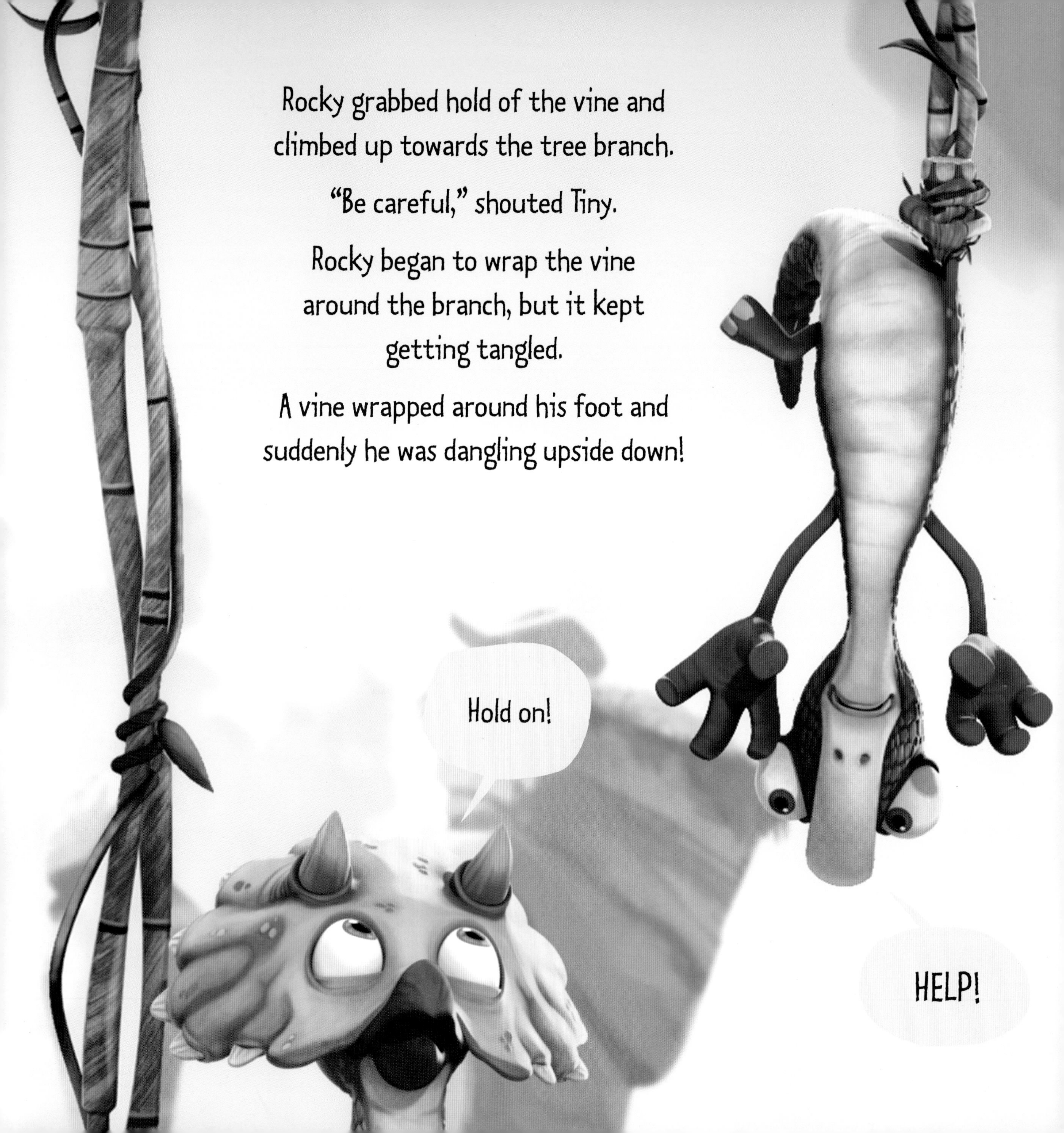

Rocky grabbed hold of the vine and climbed up towards the tree branch.

"Be careful," shouted Tiny.

Rocky began to wrap the vine around the branch, but it kept getting tangled.

A vine wrapped around his foot and suddenly he was dangling upside down!

"I've been putting everyone in danger today," said Mazu, as Bill and Tiny helped Rocky to safety.

"It's all right, Mazu," said Rocky. "We all know you're just trying to help Ayati."

Mazu sighed and got ready to try again. "Come on, we can do this!" she said to the others.

The friends climbed up the cliff and got ready to push the boulder.

"We're almost there, Ayati!" called Mazu.

"I'm not going anywhere!" she called back.

The friends pushed with all their might.

"It's too heavy!" puffed Tiny. "It won't budge!"

The little dinos rounded up the biggest, strongest dinosaurs in Cretacia, including Tiny's brother Trey, and Marshall the stegosaurus. When Mazu gave the signal everyone pushed together . . .

. . . but the boulder still wouldn't move.

"How are we going to save Ayati?" cried Mazu.

All of a sudden the ground began to RUMBLE and SHAKE . . .

ROOOAAAARRR!

"GIGANTO!" said Rocky. "He can help us!"

"That's it!" cried Mazu. "GIGANTO can push it!"

She peeped over the cliff edge. The massive dino was standing underneath a walnut tree, sniffing out his lunch.

"Hmm," said Mazu, thoughtfully. "He really does love walnuts."

Giganto had given Mazu a brilliant idea! She hitched a ride on Hegan, a flying dino with enormous wings.

"If you see a walnut, pick it up!" called Mazu.

"Giganto just knocked one loose," replied Hegan, swooping down to collect it.

Mazu gazed down hopefully. Now she just needed Giganto to follow the flying walnut!

Giganto roared as the walnut whooshed past him and he stomped after it.

"It's working!" shouted Mazu.

Mazu told Hegan to drop the walnut on the boulder.

"When Giganto goes to grab the walnut, he's sure to knock the boulder off the cliff," Mazu explained.

"How exciting!" said Rocky.

"How daring!" agreed Bill.

"What if Giganto falls off the cliff WITH the boulder?" asked Tiny.

Mazu gasped – Tiny was right! Giganto was in trouble and it was all HER fault!

"I've got to stop him!" she cried.

Hegan set Mazu down on the boulder. As Giganto stomped nearer, Mazu waved her arms desperately. They needed to help Ayati, but she didn't want to hurt Giganto in the process!

Mazu pushed the walnut towards the massive dino so he could pick it up safely.

"You did the right thing," said Rocky, as Mazu climbed back down to join the others.

Just then, they heard a crash.

Giganto had swallowed his walnut, turned to walk away – and knocked the boulder off the cliff with his tail! The weight of it falling lifted Ayati up, just like Mazu planned!

The dinosaurs cheered and Mazu smiled.
"Thanks, Giganto. I couldn't have done it without you!"

Gigantosaurus looked back and roared, then went on his way.

It was the end of another amazing day in Cretacia.

"It's good to be standing again," said Ayati. "Now I can get to the jungle before nightfall."

Mazu took out her science slate to make notes – she had learned a lot today!

"Giganto really loves walnuts," she wrote, "and helping out a big, old friend."

"Do you think that Giganto knocked the boulder off the cliff on purpose?" wondered Rocky.

"It would be nice if he did," replied Mazu.

"I know one thing," grinned Bill, "I am NOT going to ask him!"

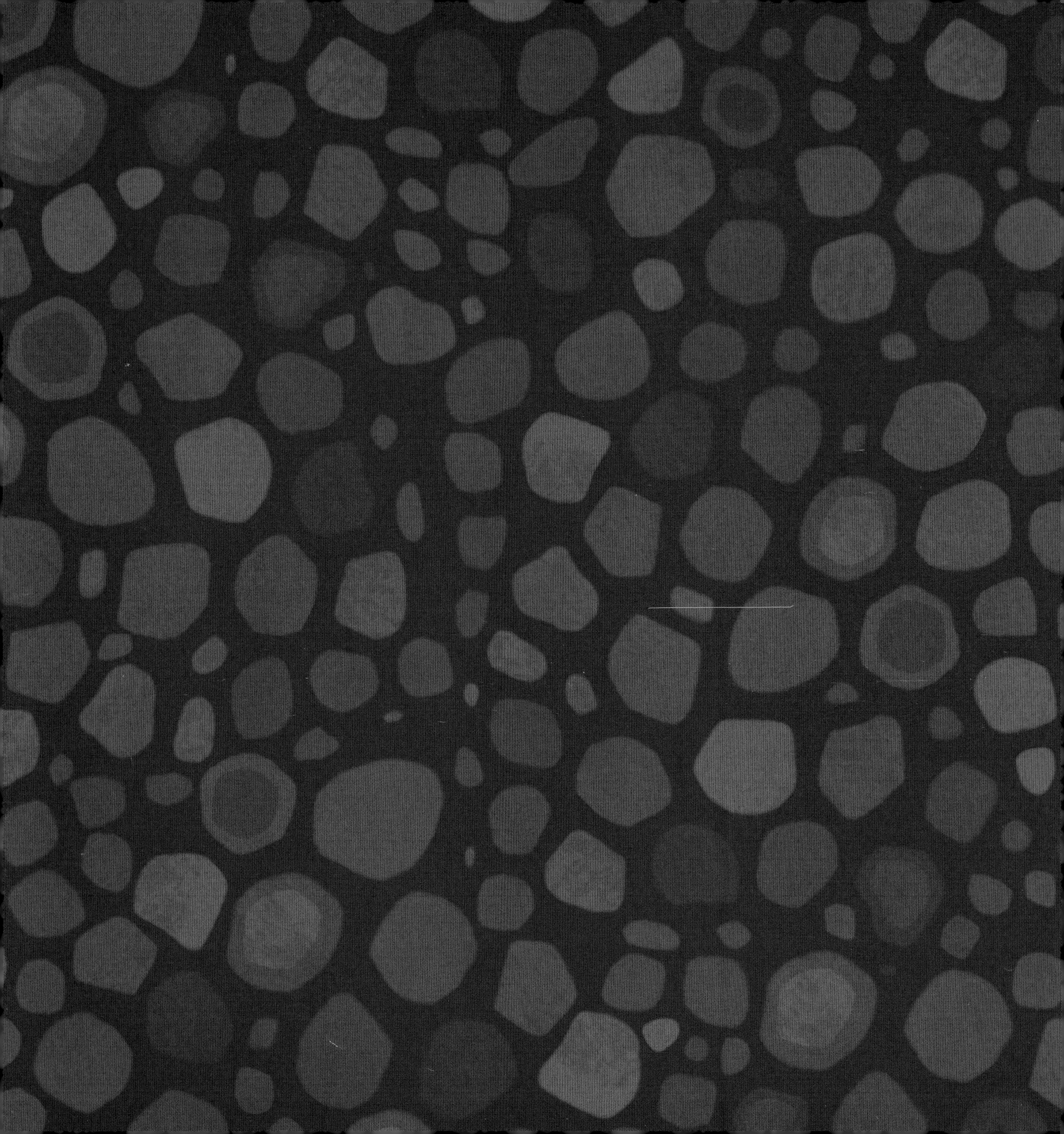